EUPHORIA

When questioned, my mother once explained to me the reason she takes so long with her goodbyes. — You will never know if it is to be your last one.

AUTHORS NOTE –

Just Like Heaven, The Cure,

Dedication:

I would like to dedicate this book to my grandmother, Nancy Rosania, of whom without, this book would not be possible. Ever since I was a little girl, she has encouraged my ambition for writing.

I love you nana, thank you for being there for me.

I would also like to thank my dear friend Lilly who deeply inspired the character Lilly Dulani.

NOTICE:

Every chapter is named after a song followed by its artist. A list has been placed on the last page of this book. I apologize in advance for any typos or grammatical errors. This entire novel was written and edited by a teenager, mostly in the wee hours of the morning.

Trigger Warnings:

Death, Eating Disorder, Night Terrors, light sexist Behaviour.

PROLOGUE-

Enterlude. The Killers.

Social Justice Topic Paper.

Psychology & Social Sciences.

Creative Essay Format.

Students: Jane Former, Lewis Pool, Joanna Lee, Dakota Mendel.

Intro:

Know this; we are not perfect. We are those who cry over chick flicks and those who fear what we do not understand. We are those who are misguided in our endeavours; we are sappy love letters etched on skin.

It could take me a million books just to tell you how I feel about life, but instead I could use a few key words. At its core, life sucks. But wrapped around that and intertwined between tanned fingers and silences broken by laughter, there is a feeling that will make every bad day worth the heart ache that comes with it. To quote Charles Bukowski,

"There is a place in the heart that will never be filled. In the best times we will know it more than ever. There is a place in the heart that will never be filled, and we will wait and wait in that place."

We will always be missing pieces, but I want you to know before we tell our stories; we are not perfect. We do not know everything, but every now and then we believe that that empty place *can* be filled. And when it is, it will be filled with *Euphoria.*

CHAPTER ONE –

Back Then, B-Story.

When we left that night, we had planned to go hiking. It was something Lilly suggested, saying how it was the perfect time of the year – It was the first of November – with the leaves the pastel pinks, reds, and oranges of autumn just barely managing to hold onto the frozen branches of winter. But, when we finally left my house, the sun had already begun to set, and the leaves were no longer very visible.

"What should we do then?" I asked, leaning my head against the truck window and eyeballing my house; green brick with off white shutters and a large cracked oak door.

"I suppose we could go grab a bite to eat." She suggested, cradling her tummy in doing so and leaning forward, causing her black hair to fall in her eyes. "Panera, maybe." She added.

I only nodded in response. I was hoping that tonight would not be as uneventful as it appeared. I hadn't seen Lilly in about two months, but she seemed to make the simplest things enjoyable. I remembered when I had just started freshmen year, and I was so nervous, so Lilly would come by, pick me up and walk me home every single day. And in the snow, she'd bring umbrellas and hot chocolate, and other treats. Lilly Dulani, 25 years old, gothic, and absolutely beautiful inside and out. She had finished High School before I had even started, but she was so young in spirit. Or maybe it was that I was so old.

For the entire ride to the restaurant, we played catch up. I hadn't seen her since summer time, and it was so nice to see her again. She had been my best friend for as long as I could remember.

"So, Jane, how's senior year treating you?" She asked, and I tried to collect a decent answer.

"Not much has happened..." I told her. I've always had a good life, but it's never been much of a story. I was new to my school, so there wasn't exactly a whole lot to report.

"Marking period 2 is about to start." I remarked dully.

~~~~~~~~~~~~~~~~~~~~~

When we were done eating, we got back in the truck and started driving. I don't know that either of us knew where we were going, or knew the full extent of what was to unfold that night, but I was more than happy to wait and find out.

At some point, the topics that had been flowing through the truck ceased, and things became quiet but not awkward. I moved my arms around slowly, my leather jacket squeaking through the silence of the car as if a testament that I had still existed beside her. She cocked her head at me, if only for a second and shot me one of those distracted but still genuine smiles.

"Where are we going?" I asked quietly, as if my voice may break the air of mystery surrounding us on that night if I dared to raise it even an octave.

"You'll see." She smiled, an excited look on her face.

I just sat back against the seat, hoping to no end that this surprise of hers would be a pleasant one. It was freezing out, and some part of me didn't like the idea of even leaving the warmth of the pick-up, but I attempted to coax myself into being just as excited as Lilly looked.

First, I had mirrored her smile, then I tried to think of all the great things we could do that night. Even though the sun had already set long ago, the evening was still very young and rich with potential.

CHAPTER TWO –

1979. Smashing Pumpkins.

When we got to our destination, I was reasonably confused. We were parked outside what seemed to be a Victorian church, with huge brick pillars up each side in perfect symmetry.

"We're…" Lilly started for me, trying to get me to guess.

"A little early for Sunday school." I joked, not quite getting where this was going just yet.

Lilly just shook her head and pulled on a pair of brown mittens, opening her door and getting out.

She's just as crazy as always, I thought. *Good crazy.* The kind of crazy that makes you feel sorry for those who are sane. I got out and followed her up to the large glass doors of the church. They had seemed to be the only new thing about the whole building, equipped with the average bolt lock.

Lilly tugged the door, but of course it was locked.

"What did you expect?" I laughed. I assumed we might get back in the nice warm truck now, and even in my long grey sweater and brown leather jacket I shivered each time the air stirred. It would be nice to re-join the heated vehicle but Lilly had other plans.

"It's locked." I told her.

"Nothings ever locked." She replied with absolute confidence.

From her tiny black bag, she produced a small pocket knife, and pressed it between the doors. It took her no more than 6 or 7 seconds of expert jiggling to undo the lock and open the door.

All at once a large, impressed smile found its way to my lips.

"You're a ninja, Lilly." I proclaimed in awe.

If she had told me she could do that, I wouldn't have doubted it, but to see her do it so expertly was a whole other story. She never ceased to amaze me.

Crazy. I thought. *Good crazy.*

~~~~~~~~~~~~~~~~~~~

Once we were inside, we walked around the large building turning on every light as we went. It was odd, I thought, to see this building in the middle of the night like it's never been seen before. I didn't doubt that this had been done before, probably to this specific church by tons of curious teenagers. But it didn't matter, for this moment it was *my* first time breaking into a church. Hell, it was my first time breaking into anywhere and it was my first adventure like this.

Lilly nudged my arm as she walked into the chapel, and I tried to memorize the way my smile felt on my face; so unstoppably fierce, like it would be there even if I didn't want it to be.

"Hey look!" I exclaimed, finding the switch that lit all the fake candles that lined the walls. *Another new thing in this old church.*

Lilly shook her head distastefully at the fake flames, all too white to be fire. "Not as gorgeous as it used to be." She told me.

I wondered if she'd done this before, maybe she broke into churches a lot. Maybe she broke into a lot of places. But she seemed to put everything back, and didn't break anything, and left no harm to the place whilst we were there, so it wouldn't surprise me if she'd never been caught, but I didn't ask. We were little ghosts, gliding through the halls of a currently uninhabited place of worship, and here, in the night, we seemed to be worshipping it in our own little ways with each held breath. Although I had never been in this particular church before, I knew I would never have been able to of seen the building in such depth if I had come for a Sunday service.

"This is nice." I told her, gaining a nod and a small contented smile from her as we explored the last few rooms in the large building.

We started walking back out, turning off the lights as we went and jumping around the pews. Eventually we were laughing pretty hard, like every word that passed the others lips was the best joke we'd ever heard.

CHAPTER THREE –

Sick Muse, Metric.

Somewhere along the walk between the church and Lilly's electric blue pick-up, we'd started talking about religion.

"I envy the hard core religious." I admitted.

"Why's that?" she laughed.

"They have things figured out. I see an awful tragedy; they see 'God Works in Mysterious Ways' or some shit." I explained.

I didn't have anything wrong with religious people, I was genuinely jealous of the life style they could lead. I'd tried it before, and it hadn't worked for me. Things could never be that simple for me.

We managed to talk enough that I didn't even think to ask where we were going next, but I had a pretty good feeling she wouldn't have told me even if I had asked.

We jumped onto the highway and got on route 78, but soon she was grumbling about how she hadn't meant to get onto this exit, and how she was getting herself lost.

"Not all that familiar with New Jersey?" I asked. She only nodded in response. We got to a traffic light and stopped.

She looked kind of adorable, her face pressed against the steering wheel, her nose scrunched up into a stink face, glaring out the front windshield as if the light was red specifically to spite her. Sometimes I thought she forgot how lucky we were to have the freedom to get lost.

~~~~~~~~~~~~~~~~~~

Eventually, I suppose she got us un-lost because before long we were yet again parked in front of a seemingly random building. But *this* time the lights were on. We got out and followed a small stone path up to the little white rectangular building.

Once I was inside, I knew exactly where I was. Or rather I seemed to know what sort of place I was in. Lilly had been a sober alcoholic for as long as I'd known her, which had been no less than six years by this point. She'd brought me along, as well as a few other people I'd known from the rooms. And since all of the buildings kind of looked the same, it didn't take me more than a few seconds to know I was in an AA meeting.

The door opened us to a room mainly dominated by a large rectangular table surrounded by mostly people in their mid-20's, like Lilly. It was a Young Peoples meeting, I gathered.

We sat down quietly, and I tried not to draw attention to myself too much. I wasn't an alcoholic, so I didn't really have any reason to say anything, but I guess they didn't know that.

One of the young men offered me a Big Book to which I attempted to decline as politely as possible.

I fidgeted nervously in my chair, looking around the room. There were 4 clocks, I noticed. Why would anyone need 4 clocks in one room? There were 4 people aside from Lilly and I, a clock for each person. Then I noticed there were 3 garbage cans, which I felt was a very large amount for such a small building, and I imagined there were more in the other 3 rooms I could spot door ways to from my seat. 4 doors, 3 garbage cans, 4 clocks, 6 people, 4 rooms, I counted things when I got nervous.

The thing that bothered me the most about the strange room we were in was an upside down photograph that read *"Think, Think, Think."* I thought it must have been done purposely, as some sort of sign there for them, but my OCD *really* didn't like it.

I glanced down at my phone to check the time.

[15]

10:23

It was getting late fast.

"You know what I noticed?" a woman at the front of the table asked, looking thoughtfully at each of us and gaining my attention.

"Hmm?" we all hummed back.

"I think that well, I don't think I can help anyone until I get myself fixed…" she started. "Or at least," she added. "Get myself taped together." I liked that, I liked that a lot. It seemed to relate to my sober life in a way I don't think she realised it could. It was a very smart, real notion and I made a mental note to remember it next time I found myself torn apart.

CHAPTER FOUR –

Here I Land, Nicholas Stevenson,

When the regular meeting had ended, we all abandoned our chairs in favour of standing in a small circle together and discussing whatever happened to pop into our heads, which when it came down to ex druggies, happened to be some very random and interesting things.

Sometimes, I thought, they were the smartest people I'd ever met. But most of the time I could tell they were all just a bunch of dumb kids, like me, who had been dealt a bad hand unlike me. I just thanked god they were here, and that I had their stories to stand testament as why I should not roll the dice to see what of my families genes had been passed down to me.

"How many years you got, Hun?" one of them asked me, and I could see Lilly smiling out of the corner of my eye.

I always made jokes about the looks I'd get when I told them I wasn't an alcoholic. Some people smiled and congratulated me, some thanked me for accompanying my friends who were alcoholics, and some gave me a weird look as if I had just released to the public that I missed the qualification it took to be part of their club.

Thank goodness though; these people seemed quite genuinely good-natured.

"Never had too much trouble with addiction, myself." I told him.

"Good." he replied.

"Don't change." another boy added.

"I won't." I assured them.

I'd seen this disease wipe out families, ruin relationships, and kill more than its fair share of beautiful people. And that, on a point of principle, was not something I wanted to get myself involved with at any point in this world or the next.

Slowly, one by one, each person excused themselves from the room. They all shook Lilly's hand and then mine, and reminded me not to change.

"Stay like this." the woman said to me as she left "It's good." She added.

~~~~~~~~~~~~~~~~~~

Lilly and I were the last to leave, and just making the trip back to the truck nearly froze my ears, so I tugged my short locks of brown hair down into my face and flipped up my collar.

"How are you surviving out here in just that?" I asked Lilly.

She shrugged and lifted her mitten clad hands "They're warm." she laughed.

She was only in a thin brown sweater and a pair of jeans, and just looking at her made me shiver. I would have already frozen.

CHAPTER FIVE –

Wonderwall, Oasis,

"Almost to our next stop!" Lilly announced after a few minutes of driving. Her eyes were full of happiness, an icy cool joy like steal flowers.

I glanced to the clock on the radio and blue squared numbers blinked at me:

11:46

But somehow I knew that was wrong, so I fished around in my pocket and found my phone.

Correction: it was 12:46am.

Late night meetings were always nice, I thought. I couldn't help wondering where we'd go next. Maybe we'd grab some coffee, I thought, supressing a yawn. I was a bit tired, but in no hurry to go home to my boring house with my all too uncomfortable bed.

"Where are we going?" I asked.

"It's a surprise." she answered.

"What are we going to do there?"

"Hit the books." she told me, tapping her steering wheel with her, still mitten clad, left hand.

I shook my head at her. I hadn't known where I was going or what I was doing since dinner, and although I usually hated not having control over myself, at the moment I was ok with it. Lilly had a talent of making everything feel light. She had a real burning hot knack for making everything okay... and the funniest thing was I don't even think she knew when she was doing it.

~~~~~~~~~~~~~~~~~~

After about 15 minutes more of driving, we had entered Allentown PA, and parked outside a local library.

Part of me wanted to tell Lilly that it was closed, but I knew by then that those sorts of things were not to apply to us, not on that night. So, instead, I sighed and hopped out of the truck first this time.

When I got up to the front entrance, I jiggled the handle just to humour myself and then stepped aside for Lilly. Once again, she produced a small pocket knife from her little purse and jimmied the lock open.

I couldn't help but wonder where she'd learned that, but before I could do too much wondering, Lilly was pulling me through the big white medal door frame and into one of the places I had spent most of my high school career. But this time, of course, it was different. Everything was different this late at night, like the way the moonlight hit the books and made everything look like a black and white Tumblr post. And it was beautiful.

"I love books," Lilly told me, sighing happily, a smile plastered on her face. "They're friends."

I smiled at that and added, "They're teleports."

"Time machines." she offered.

"Proof."

"Of what?" she asked.

"Proof that mere mortals can make magic." I replied, running my finger across a line of young adult fiction.

"Hm…" Lilly hummed, as if thinking about what I'd said. "I don't believe Rolling was a mere mortal." She giggled.

I couldn't help but giggle back.

"Don't you write?" she asked.

My cheeks got a little pink, but I counted on the cold weather to cover that up.

"I used to but I'm no good at it anymore." I explained, swallowing hard. "I haven't really tried to write anything lately, though." I admitted.

"You should." she told me, finally finding the light switch.

Now I could see the rows and rows of books, magnificent pieces of lives both fictional and non-fictional alike, spread out in front of us like a mosaic.

"I could understand breaking into a church; you usually never have an opportunity to explore the church like we did." I said. "But why did we break into a library? What can we do now we couldn't do in the morning?"

Lilly gave me a sly smile and took a long, exaggerated breath. And then, louder than I thought possible, she screamed. Well, more of a squeal, a happy squeal.

"**No shushing librarians!**" she yelled.

My lips crinkled into an open smile, and I couldn't help myself. I bellowed out my loudest most un-restrained scream, knowing very well the houses nearby could call the police if they heard us, but relying on the hope that they wouldn't.

"**I can read looking for Alaska <u>out loud!</u>**" I screeched.

"**Nerd!**" Lilly replied.

I knew it was weird, but screaming in a library felt like one of the best things I had ever done in my entire life.

CHAPTER SIX –

Outgrown, Best Left Unsaid,

Eventually, we decided to put all the books back and leave. We had spent what felt like hours screaming happily at one another from opposite sides of the library. We recited loud excerpts of our favourite books; along with ones we'd never read, new and old. Sometimes they had been serious, and other times they were accompanied by silly voices and terrible accents. *From here on*, I thought, *any average trip to the library will pale in comparison to the memory of this night.*

On our way out, Lilly relocked the door, the red light of the glowing exit sign bouncing off the sunglasses on top of her head. I wondered, briefly, why she had put them on in the first place whilst getting ready to come out this evening. They sat on top of her head, pushing back her black hair like a head band.

The truck, despite being unmanned for such a long time, was still dramatically warmer than the air surrounding it when we got back in. It was filled with the upmost joy, some sort of raw euphoria slipping into us like a drug via breaths taken. It was the most pure and beautiful happiness I had ever felt and I doubted very much I'd ever feel it again.

"Next stop?" I asked.

"Bringing you home, kiddo." Lilly teased with a small hint of empathy hiding beneath the smile on her face.

The smile was a large, peach, crescent moon spread out across the pale sky that was her face.

"Awe…" I cooed. I didn't want the night to end, but I was tired. One glance at the clock convinced me.

5:45am

The night had all but ended in a physical sense, and it would probably be a good idea to end on such a good note, anyway.

"Alright." I sighed, traces of a yawn working its way into my voice like an infection.

And like an infection, it spread. Soon Lilly was yawning too, and we had delved into a conversation about comfort foods.

"I can make some mean chocolate pudding." she told me, giggling.

"I can too." I told her, boastfully. "So long as it comes in a box and has some step by step instructions."

We talked like that for the whole ride to my house, and when we got there she parked out in front of it and turned to me, tucking her long hair behind her ears and offering me a sweet look.

"Thanks for coming."

"Thanks for having me."

I opened the truck door then, and I felt as though I was seeing my house for the first time in days, maybe weeks. The shudders seemed dirtier in the dusk and the sun peaking over the hills made the green look more like emerald. Lilly pulled on the sleeve of my jacket as I stood up and I turned slowly to her.

"Yeah?" I asked.

"We're going to do this more often, right?" she asked excitedly.

"You're there I'm there." I told her with a laugh. "And hey," I added. "We still haven't gone hiking."

I turned back around and closed the car door, tapping my hand off the window and ambling lazily up the few steps of my porch, wanting to draw out the night as long as I could.

~~~~~~~~~~~~~~~~~~

When I got inside, I walked through my living room to the stairs, taking them two at a time up to my bedroom where I threw myself on my bed and passed out. My dreams were sure to be riddled with every variation of the events that had occurred that night.

Tonight was worth dreaming about.

CHAPTER SEVEN –

Jesus Christ, Brand New,

When the sun pushed through the large rectangular window on the opposite side of my bedroom, I was wrapped in the last remaining bits of that euphoric feeling I had been soaking up the night before, in the car.

There was something about the sun on that morning, like an omen. It was bright white and encompassing like it was trying to whitewash my bedroom walls and me right along with them, into nothing.

As I sat up, I wrapped the covers around my shoulders and rubbed the sleep from my eyes. It was at that point, that the phone rang.

Don't You by *Simple Minds* rung out in the silent bedroom like a siren. I fumbled around in my blankets and quickly found my cell phone. Unknown Name was written across the caller ID slot.

"Hm..." I hummed, wondering if I should answer.

In the end, I did, pressing the phone up against my head.

"Hello?" I greeted, making it more of a question. *Who is this? What do you want? Why are you calling me at 8am?*

The voice that answered was calm, collected, but sympathetic at first.

"Jane, it's Mika, Lilly's roommate." she told me, and now it sounded like she wanted to cry, but I could tell she was trying her best not to.

I couldn't help but let my mind wonder through the reasons why Mika would call me and also where she had found my number. I knew Mika, but only through Lilly. They had attended the same university and lived together since their sophomore year.

"What's going on?" I asked.

Her voice did break then, like it was giving out under some extreme force. She was an end table trying to hold up Christmas dinner.

"Lilly." she quivered out.

I nearly dropped the phone, nearly hung up all together. My mind flooded with things that could be wrong. I brought my phone a few inches from my head to check my messages, and there were none from Lilly. She had promised to text me when she got home safe.

Why hadn't she gotten home safe? Where was she? What happened? I wanted to ask all of these things but instead I just sat there like an idiot, my tongue incorrigible and useless.

"What about her?" I finally managed to stutter out. "I was out with her last evening." I added, trying to stay hopeful that this was all one big error in communication, or a practical joke.

Mika took a large shaking breath, like she was about to submerge herself in water. "Lilly." she began again and I could practically hear her stirring her words, trying to see which ones tasted too sick in her mouth before she fed them to me. "She's gone." she finally stuttered out.

The sun continued to gleam through my window; bathing the room like a white ocean and on my bed I took refuge from the waves.

Now there were tears falling down my cheeks like silver raindrops, pooling at the tip of my chin and threatening to spill over into my lap.

"Wha-what do you mean? Did she not come home last night?" *she's probably just at a friend's place* I assured myself. *Or maybe her car broke down.*

"No…" Mika sighed, like she didn't know if she could speak above a whisper without breaking down. "Jane," she started, "Jane, there's been an accident."

CHAPTER EIGHT –

The Night I Drove Alone, Citizen.

It had been a week since Lilly died. They told me that she hit a patch of ice on the way home from dropping me off. And I can't help but feel this sick guilt in my stomach like I wish I could have done something, wish I could have been the one to do the driving that night.

The funeral procession was quiet, and still. I have a feeling that's how all funerals look, though. I remember thinking how Lilly would want us to be screaming and reading scripture. She wouldn't want this silence. But to quote John Green, *Funerals are for the living.*

It was held in the same church we'd broken into 3 days before, but the feelings were all wrong. I could barely recognise the place when I saw it in the morning light, and I couldn't help but notice this emptiness growing in the pit of my stomach like a black whole sucking up every last scrap of joy that I could manage to hold on to.

When Mika approached me, I had successfully found a corner to scrunch up in. My brown hair was pinned out of my eyes, my leather jacket and grey sweater replaced now by a black dress, my boots now black flats.

The curtains lining the casket were lavender with black roses. I couldn't help but cringe at the thought of why the lid was closed. How bad had the crash been? What was the exact thing that killed her? I was too afraid to ask and besides, I knew it would only make the nightmares more vivid.

Mika had asked me to say a few words, but I couldn't. I couldn't even speak right then and there in front of her. I only shook my head, tears re-joining my skin and stinging my eyes. *Lilly would understand.* I assured myself. *Wouldn't she?*

The women from the young people's meeting had been there, hearing from others of her passing.

They all looked like they had been deprived of oxygen, all small gasps and white faces.

~~~~~~~~~~~~~~~~~~~~~~~~~~~~~~~~~~~~~~~

When I missed the first few days of school, no one called home. The High School gives you about 3 days excused if it's not a family death. I had decided to take the week off, and I spent the majority of it sleeping and watching crappy old movies in an attempt to get my mind off Lilly.

But eventually I felt like I had to go back. I had to get myself taped together.

"You don't have to if you're not ready." my mother had said, looking at me with sympathy in her eyes.

"If I don't I'm going to fail all my classes." I explained, straightening my baby blue jeans and buttoning them.

It's not that I was particularly stoked to go back to Leviathan High, with its dirty bathrooms and second rate education but I sure as hell didn't want to fail either.

I was looking in the mirror, studying my face carefully trying to hold back the tears that were constantly threatening to spill over. My brown hair was getting longer, tickling the back of my neck at this point, and my skin looked tan despite the fact that I barely went outside anymore. My shirt was a plane white T, only serving to make me look even more tan and I had applied a small bit of eyeliner to my top lid.

"Well if you are going –" my mother explained tentatively. "You'd best be off soon."

CHAPTER NINE –

Of a Friday Night. Anaïs Mitchell.

When I got to school, I could feel eyes on me like daggers in my skin, so I pulled my hood up and hurried to my first period class.

At first, the day had been uneventful and full of *'I heard you lost someone, I'm so sorry'* and every word felt so utterly meaningless I couldn't help but wonder why they even tried. I tried to say thank you, I knew they meant well, but something about losing someone makes you bitter like there's no way anyone can understand what you're going through. That's how Mrs. Culp, the school grief consoler, explained it.

~~~~~~~~~~~~~~~~~~~~~~~~~~~~~~~~~~~

"Now Jane, I know you're going to have a very trifling time readjusting to school life after such a tremendous loss, your mother tells us you've known Lilly for the better part of your life – isn't that right?" Mrs. Culp asked; her voice cool and clinical.

"That's right." I agreed. I stood up to leave, realising that the lunch period we had used to talk about this was nearly over. "Now if that's all..." I added. "I'd better be off to class."

"Oh yes of course, tell us if you need anything, dear." She told me, a smile just barely lacing her lips as she turned back to her key board and immediately returned to whatever work a grief counsellor does.

~~~~~~~~~~~~~~~~~~~~

My last class of the day was an elective called Psychology and Social Sciences, but we all called it S3; which I found to make no grammatical sense but it was catchy.

"Hello kids and congratulations. Welcome to your final marking period in my class. The semester ends after this marking period and you will be moving on to other electives." Mr. Sapir began.

He was always drawing everything out with a small smile and an antidote that had little to no relevance.

"If any of your friends have ever taken my senior class, they've probably told you all about the final project that I'm going to talk to you about today." He gestured to the slide show he had up on the smart board entitled 'FINAL'

As he continued, my mind drifter somewhere else. My wooden desk felt warm under my hands and it was easy to rest my head on it. I hadn't gotten much sleep so I needed the rest.

"Wouldn't you agree, Miss Former?" Mr. Sapir asked, calling me by my last name, and I snapped my attention back up to the front.

"I'm sorry, can you repeat the question?" I asked expertly.

"We're all so excited for me to assign groups." he explained, and I could only shake my head in response, gaining a few giggles.

I hated group assignments, and once more I didn't have a clue what this assignment even was.

"Mr. S!" the boy beside me exclaimed. "Can we pick our own partners?" he asked, eyeballing a girl behind me.

"No, Lewis." Mr. Sapir said flatly. "I'll post groups on the school website tonight. You'll have most of the marking period to find a Social Justice topic, get it approved with me, and find a way of preforming the assignment for the class." he said, now facing the whole class once more. "This project gives you kids a lot of freedom, I expect great things."

[38]

The bell rang after a few more minutes of discussion, and he passed out some papers detailing the assignment. I left the class with my head down and my ear buds in.

How the hell was I supposed to deal with something like this?

CHAPTER TEN –

Brothers on a Hotel Bed. Death Cab for Cutie.

When I got home, I opened my laptop and logged onto the school website. I found the page for postings and periodically refreshed it, playing Sonic Adventures on my hand held and munching on a protein bar. I hadn't gotten a chance to eat anything because of the meeting with the grief counsellor, but then again I hadn't been all that hungry since The Accident.

I had caught myself calling it that, *The Accident*, with a capital T and A, like some vague medical experiment gone wrong. But it was better then what everyone else would call it. Even Mika called it *Lilly*. *"Ever since Lilly, I can't sleep."* They'd say. But I couldn't reduce her name down to that meaning. Before, Lilly had been so much more to these people but after she died her name represented her absence. I didn't want that.

I refreshed again, and this time a link was up on the page. I clicked it and it brought me to another page lined with everyone's school ID pictures of every senior S3 student. It took me a minute to find my own, and I cringed when I saw it. I don't think anyone ever likes their school pictures.

Jane Former

Senior

GROUP

I clicked group, and it opened a tab with more names and faces.

Dakota Mendel

He looked vaguely familiar, a tall lanky boy with too much hair grease.

Joanna Lee

She wasn't ringing a bell, but she looked sweet. She had lacy black hair that fell in her face and wore a small red tank top in her picture.

I scrolled down to find the last partner.

Lewis Pool

I cringed again. The boy from class, he'd been the one eyeballing the poor girl behind me. I knew him too well. He was a sexist, narcissistic bastard. And now I had to be in a group with him.

I growled audibly under my breath and made a note of my partner's names in a small notebook I kept beside my bed. I took a moment to memorize their faces, closed the tab, and re-joined some cliché 1990's American movie about high school life that I had been watching the night before.

I couldn't help but think to myself as I sat there, watching as the main character walked up the long expanse of the school halls, that the movies most certainly had it all wrong. School was never really like this, life was never really like this. Never this simple.

~~~~~~

That night, I had a nightmare. Lilly was there, and she was asking me why I had let her die. In the dream, I had frozen up and no matter how hard I tried I couldn't answer her. I watched her die over and over in a million bloody ways and it wouldn't stop.

When I woke up, my mother had me sitting up in bed and was currently gently rubbing the small of my back.

"It's okay, it's okay." She repeated soothingly, and pulled me into a hug.

"I'm so stupid. I let her die." I told her. I knew it wasn't true, but the dream had made me all funny. I couldn't stop shaking.

"Jane, you didn't let her die, and you are most certainly not stupid." She protested all matter-of-fact-like.

"Yes I am." I told her, burying my face into the crook of her neck. I was balling like a child at that point. I wanted to curl into her and disappear.

"Hun, you are smart..." she started. "You're so bright, you could teach the stars a thing or two about shining"

CHAPTER ELEVEN –

Too Much Time, John Vanderslice.

When I woke up the next day, I was still in that midway point between being asleep and awake, where you can't remember all the things you would rather forget. My phone was blaring *Toxic by Britany Spears*, and I was just conscious enough to remember how outdated the song was.

"**Jane get up!**" my mother yelled up the stairs, and that pulled me out of my daze.

My mother was at the foot of my bed now, her brunet hair accompanied by blonde streaks hanging down into her face messily, a toothbrush hanging out of her mouth. She was in her office clothes.

"You need to get up now." she repeated, her voice muffled against her tooth brush.

I pulled myself into a sitting position and yawned. Now I could remember all the things I'd rather forget and now I didn't want to get up. I plopped myself back down, pulling the covers around me like a cocoon and praying to nothing that my mother would let me stay home.

"Jane," she huffed, taking the toothbrush out of her mouth for a moment. "You need to go to school or you'll fail this term, you said it yourself now get up."

I didn't want to get up. I didn't want to go to school and have to see my group partners. I hadn't even bothered to read the papers and figure out what exactly a *Social Justice Topic* was.

I whined uneasily and rolled out of bed, giving my mother a look that asked her to leave so that I could get dress. Once she did I found the blue jeans I'd worn the day before and a long sleeved green dress shirt, pulling my winter jacket over it.

When I looked out the window I saw snow puffing down, red leaves just barely clinging to the frozen trees, so I pulled on some woolly black gloves as well.

Every morning I'd wake up with this feeling like I needed to go find Lilly. *Where are you?* I thought.

~~~~~~~~~~~~~~~~~~~~~~~~~~~~~~~~~~~~

The bus was late, leaving me to stand in the snow for about 10 minutes, my breath making clouds in the air. I kicked at the snow, already sticking to the ground and knocking down the remaining leaves that hung from the trees. It was so quiet and the tiny town seemed to be just starting to wake up as the bus pulled up almost silently.

"Hey." I greeted to the girl beside me as I took my seat.

"Morning." she whispered back.

There was something about the storm that made everything hushes, and we couldn't help but hush along with the rest of the world. Even the rowdy kids in the back of the bus seemed to of gotten the memo.

Leaning back against the seat, I pulled my S3 papers out and started reading about the project.

'Hello class of 2014! With this being the final marking period of your time here with me in Psychology and Social Sciences, I am obligated to provide you with a Final project. –'

I skimmed lazily through the rest of the introduction; I wanted to figure out what this was really all about.

'– In this project you and 3-4 other students will be asked to pick a <u>Social Justice Topic</u>. An SJT is a topic regarding social or psychological problems and the solutions to those problems. For example,

many students choose to do there's on something like racism but you may also choose something like suicide, women's rights, or the deeper meanings of life. These are all things that still effects people today, and comes with many solutions and side effects —'

I sighed; there was a lot to read but not that many rules. He was pretty much giving us free reign of this project and letting us do whatever we wanted with it. I could see myself having a lot of fun with it if I wasn't stuck doing it with a group.

Lewis would never let us do feminism. He'd be an ass the whole time. *Hell, he'll probably be an ass the whole time regardless.* I thought.

CHAPTER TWELVE –

At Least I Have Nothing, Saints Motel

I was officially convinced that Mr. S was the only teacher giving the seniors any work. Usually senior year was mostly lax, with easy to pass quizzes and no homework. It was mostly reviewing and studying for final tests, they didn't really have a lot of new things to teach us. But Sapir wanted to pile as much heat on this project as he could.

"Who here knows exactly which college they'll be in next year?" he asked us at the beginning of class, sitting on the front of his desk.

Some of the class raised their hands. I didn't. I didn't know what I wanted yet and it was killing me to be honest.

"Well to the people who haven't, the final project always looks good on a college application form." He told the class, smiling like he had just given us a present.

I laid my head on the desk briefly, feeling waves of exhaustion rolling over me.

In the room there were 4 Lord of the Rings figures on Mr. Sapir's desk, 32 students, 1 teacher, 1 exit, 5 windows, and 1 closet.

"I know you all want to get to the project" Mr. Sapir teased. "So, for anyone who didn't check I shall now announce the groups and tell you how you are expected to get together."

There was a round of groans in reply, and I could tell I was far from the only one dreading this. The groans continued as he began reading off names. When he got to my name, I felt a pang of hope that maybe the list had been wrong. But sure enough, it was the same.

"Jane Former

Lewis Pool

Joanna Lee

Dakota Mendel"

Lewis growled and slammed his head on the desk.

"Please go and sit with your groups." the teacher told us.

Lewis moved his desk around to face me like it hurt him to do it. Dakota and Joanna joined us soon after, Dakota staring down at his converse sheepishly and Joanna sporting a perky smile.

[49]

"Hey there." she greeted, giving us each our very own individual adoring glances. She was very bubbly, in that annoying kind of way where you want to hate her for it but you can't seem to bring yourself to.

She pushed her raven black hair up out of her tanned face into a pony tail and took out a neon blue binder with *'S3'* written across it. Joanna was half Caucasian half Asian, but that's all I knew. I also knew she was beautiful, and I found myself staring at her a bit, and snapped out of it quickly.

"Hi." Dakota answered meekly, running his fingers through his greasy dark brown hair and picking at the hem of his Band T.

I couldn't recognize the band, and the font was very hard to read, but it appeared to say **Biblical Violence** under what looked like a bible with a knife stabbed through it. I nearly giggled out loud when I noticed the silver cross around his neck. Either he was the next slayer, or his music taste didn't collide well with his religion.

Dakota and Lewis fist bumped like 5th graders and nodded toward one another. I hadn't really seen them talk much in class, but I'd seen them sitting on the bus together talking about video games.

"Hola." I greeted, pronouncing the H excessively, just to clear up the language confusion my dark skin tone seemed to set. *I'm Brazilian or something,* I thought. *Not Spanish.*

"Yeah yeah we've all met!" Lewis growled. He was wearing his football uniform, and his bleach blonde hair was spiked up in a way that looked sharp to the touch. His jersey hung loosely on his neck, and his skin was a sweet pale colour. He was actually sort of attractive... until he opened his mouth. It was a pity.

Joanna's smile faltered a bit in Lewis's direction and then recovered.

"Ok class," Mr. S started again "Now that you're in your groups, please discuss how you will be meeting up to complete this project. The class time I give you, although generous, will be extremely minimal."

The class groaned again in response, and I resisted the urge to smack my head off the desk, like Lewis had done. But then I remembered that unlike Lewis, I had a brain to protect.

"Let's meet at my place." Lewis offered, smiling at Joanna.

"Let's not and say we did." She said back. Such a cocky sentence and yet she still managed to make it sound like one of the sweetest things she could have said

"How about a café?" Joanna offered. And Dakota shook his head in disagreement.

I felt like taking charge then, realising that if I was to be stuck in this group, I was not about to let them fail me.

"Here's how it's going to work." I told them, and they looked at me like they were just now realising that I was sat there at all. "We're going to take turns picking public places to meet up at. Nowhere too loud, and there needs to be room for actual working. AKA; a table and some chairs."

They nodded in response.

"Why don't you pick first, Joanna?" I offered, trying to sound at least half as sweet as she looked.

"Okay." she agreed

We sat around discussing where to go, what to bring, and what to do when we got there. Joanna took notes in her blue binder as we talked.

"We won't have any class time until next week." Dakota told us, "so we'll pick back up when we all meet."

Here we go.

CHAPTER THIRTEEN –

Kill a Hipster, Watsky

I wasn't surprised when Joanna wanted us to meet at Starbucks, she had that stereotypical hipster vibe to her and I was not all that upset with the idea either. There's plenty of space to work, I knew they wouldn't get upset with us for loitering, and they've got Wi-Fi.

The next few days were more or less uneventful, and when Saturday came I was almost excited for the change of pace. We'd all exchanged numbers, so I'd woken to a text from Dakota asking me if I could bring a laptop since his mother was borrowing his. I sat up and glared at the half broken PC on the opposite side of the room. It was adorn with sticker and random sharpie markings.

Sure thing. I texted back

I stood in front of my mirror and starred at the bags under my eyes, I hadn't been sleeping a lot lately.

~~~~~~

My ma had a business meeting, so I had to walk to Starbucks. She's the CEO of some holistic medicine corporation that teaches us everything from *ginger in your tea can help a cold* to *eat this plant! Now you don't have cancer!* I knew the first one all too well. But if it proves anything, no one in our family ever got sick.

As I walked to Starbucks, my backpack hitting against my hip with every step, I thought about all the ideas I'd had for the final project topic. I tried not to get too ahead of myself; we had to work through the details together before anyone could suggest anything. And besides, I was pretty scared they'd shoot down all my ideas anyway.

When I turned down the next road, I could see Starbucks. It didn't look too full, which comforted me. I wasn't very fond of large crowds. But before I could psych myself out, I was already there. I could see Joanna inside, in a barista uniform, her apron thrown over the back of her chair and her long black hair pinned back swiftly. Her skin was especially golden with the light coming through the window and I had to remind myself not to stare as I walked through the door.

"Jane!" she exclaimed happily, loud enough for a few people to look up from their lap tops and hot drinks.

The way Joanna talked to me made me feel special, and she was so pretty and nice that it just made it feel like that much more of an honour. I would think she was flirting with me if I hadn't seen her talked to a billion other people just like this. It wasn't that she was trying to get everyone to fall in love with her, that's just how it worked out.

"Hey." I greeted lamely, setting my bag on the table and pulling my crappy laptop from it.

"How are you?" she asked, like she really did want to know

"I'm grand." I replied, and I flashed her a small smile.

Her smile twitched like she didn't believe me, but she quickly brushed it off. I really didn't like when her smile left her face, even just for that moment. I noticed that when she wasn't smiling, which was rare, she didn't look as beautiful. I mean, she still looked absolutely gorgeous, but when she smiled she looked like something that can only be born out of Photoshop. She made everyone else look crappy in comparison.

"I got you a brown sugar cinnamon coffee with no sugar." she told me. "You can add sugar, but I didn't know if maybe you took Splenda."

I smiled and nodded. "Thank you."

"No problem." she told me, swaying her hand forward like she was knocking down my thank you.

She pointed to one of the two coffees on the table. I took it nervously and went to get some sugar from the front.

By time I had returned to the table, Dakota was there. He was wearing a tight black T shirt with tons of bracelets up his arms, his hair swept back in its usual Arctic Moneys style. *Plenty of grease* I thought. I couldn't help but wonder if he applied it or made his own.

"Hey, dude." I greeted, raising my coffee cup in his direction. He nodded back, pulling the headphones out of his ears.

There was an aura of awkwardness around us, like no one knew what to say and we couldn't start working until Lewis got there. No one was surprised that he was late.

Dakota pulled my laptop in front of him and opened it.

"Hey." I whined. "Ask first."

"Fine." he laughed. He had a nice laugh, full and deep. "May I?" he asked in an overly polite tone.

Joanna giggled and took a sip of her coffee; scribbling god knows what into her binder.

"Yes you may." I replied, leaning into my chair and folding my arms.

Dakota laughed and had me log in.

"What's funny?" Joanna asked him, leaning across the table still scribbling.

"This computer is such shit. All it's got is old video games, Photoshop, and Microsoft Word." he was laughing like he hadn't said the punch line yet "It's such an outdated Word too!" he added finally.

I tore my laptop from his hands and opened up Google Chrome. "Shush." I told him.

Just then, Lewis pushed through the front door in a grey T-Shirt and some loose fitting blue jeans, his hair for once not spiked. When he sat down he fist bumped Dakota and gave Joanna and I a cocky smile. His smiles differed from Joanna's greatly. Hers made you feel loved, his made you feel abused.

CHAPTER FOURTEEN –

Walls, Oklahoma Car Crash,

We didn't do very much, I set up a template for our notes and Joanna and Lewis took turns reading through the examples done by students in the years past. I counted all the wall tiles and costumers. We decided that we'd spend the next few days' brain storming, and then I would get to pick a time and a place to meet up after school on Tuesday.

So that meant I had Sunday to myself. I considered spending the day researching topics, but I had no motivation. My mother went out with her friend for the day and I had no siblings, so nothing was stopping me from lying around all day. So that's what I did.

When I woke up, my mother was already gone. I sat up groggily just to flop back down, exhausted. I looked over to the alarm clock on my bedside table, staring through the sleep in my eyes trying to decipher the numbers.

2:31pm

Great I thought to myself, rolling over and staring at my tiny bedroom. The walls were a clean white, the floor adorn with black carpet and all the furniture was wooden. I had a small desk with a roll top where I spent many late nights, which had been currently open sporting a large notebook I used to use for writing.

I suddenly realised how long it had been since I had sat at my own desk. My eyes continued to scan the room. I sucked at most instruments, and a loan black electric guitar was leaned back in its stand beside the dresser, opposite to the desk. The only instrument I had ever been any good at was the piano, but we couldn't afford a real one so the closest thing I had was a crummy key board lying next to the book shelf.

My book shelf had always been over flowing. It had everything from John Green to Shakespeare, and I had read it all a million times.

Eventually, I climbed out of bed and slipped on my largest pair of sweat pants, tucking my loose T-Shirt into it. I pulled the stool out from under my desk and sat down, wrenching open my laptop and cracking my knuckles.

I could hear Lilly in my head like a faint whisper.

"Don't you write?" she had asked.

"I used to. But I'm no good at it anymore. Haven't really tried to write anything lately, though." I answered.

"You should." she had told me,

I continued to think of her as I opened and my outdated Microsoft word

And the mental image of her smiling face very nearly broke my heart.

~~~~~~

When I finally closed my laptop and pulled the desk top shut, the tic tack of my keys finally ceasing, it was already dark outside. My mother had gotten home hours ago and offered me some Chinese, but I was too busy to be hungry.

"You have to eat something." she had told me, but I shook her off.

"I will." I promised. "Just not right now."

She nodded reluctantly and walked back down the stairs. I had an attic bedroom, and if you tried walking too far in any direction the ceiling would come down to meet you. I had my own flight of stairs and a door without a handle. We lived in a ranch house, so they didn't count this as another floor. Ma had a bedroom downstairs and we had a dinky living room with a large TV we'd watch dumb life time movies on whenever one of us was sad.

It was only 9pm when I climbed into bed and passed out beneath the duvet.

CHAPTER FIFTEEN—

Come on Eileen, Dexys Midnight Runners.

Monday, like most Mondays, went by slowly and in the most boring fashion. Classes glazed by, tedious pages of all too easy homework was assigned and finished before the bell even rang. When last period came, however, I had art class.

I had worn my black jeans and one of my many crew neck T-Shirts that day, and I felt a bit cold as I entered the draftee room. The art teacher smiled happily toward me as I entered.

"Morning, Jane." Ms. Doll called, organizing a box of sharpies as she talked.

I smiled in response, nodding and sitting down at my table. We were working on a pencil sketch project entitled *'Wish Upon a Dream'* where we were all asked to sketch out the one thing we desired more than anything else. It was a difficult project, because I had always been pretty contented with what I had, and when I wasn't contented, I wanted too many things at all sorts of levels.

I wondered if I should draw Lilly, but it needed to be an inanimate object or an idea. I had decided to sketch a large pepperoni pizza. But that had most likely been because I had not eaten at all that day; aside from a handful of grapes.

"Nice work, dude." a voice from my left said happily.

I looked up to see who it was. A girl with a mocha skin tone and a nearly buzzed hair cut stood before me, sporting a baby blue dress and some matching blue heels. She was beautiful.

"Th-thanks." I managed to stutter out sheepishly.

Now that I was really looking at her, and seeing her dark emerald eyes, I recognized her. She sat on the far side of the room and drew the most beautiful things. She was perhaps the best in our whole school.

"Mind if I work here today?" she asked, gesturing her half-finished sketch papers in the direction of the empty drawing desk beside me.

"Sure." I replied shortly, smiling up at her as she took the seat. She was absolutely breath taking.

We worked in silence for a few minutes, and then she began to whisper little jokes to me.

"Where did the Cyber man leave his spaceship?" she asked, suppressing giggles.

"Where?" I asked.

"The parking meteor!" she exclaimed, a smile stretching across her face.

A small laugh escaped my lips and I tried to think of the perfect way to describe her smile.

Ralph Waldo Emerson said it perfectly I thought, *she had a smile as wide as hope.*

CHAPTER SIXTEEN –

Sloppy Seconds, Watsky.

Tuesday afternoon was finally upon us and I had decided to meet everyone at the library, a reasonable choice I thought.

I texted everyone directions to the one in Allentown I had gone to with Lilly. Seeing it in the daytime was even stranger than seeing the church. When I approached the door I half expected it to be locked, but I remembered quickly that it was day time now. And if the door had been locked, I didn't have Lilly's little pocket knife. I didn't have Lilly.

The cold air stung my throat and froze my lips, so finally, I went in. The library was larger than I had realized that night, and when I walked among the large stacks of books I felt an unbelievable sense of vertigo.

I reserved a circular table for us off in the back and opened my computer. I hadn't thought very much about the group project over the days we were supposed to brain storm, but I had a plan.

"Hey Jane." Dakota muttered under his breath. He had a large woolly jumper on, and looked pale and cold and just as awkward and greasy as always.

"Hey dude." I replied coolly, kicking a chair out for him.

He sat and pulled open his backpack, removing a large Alienware laptop. My mouth gapped.

"C'mon Dakota." I whined. "My laptop already looked like shit before you put that beauty right next to it!"

He laughed and shook his head at me. "Got any topic ideas?" he asked, turning the machine before him on with a click.

I only nodded; I wanted to wait until the others got here before I shared.

"I don't have shit." he laughed again, a low baritone that just didn't fit with his scrawny physique.

I noticed Joanna wondering around looking for us and waved my hand around in the air to get her attention. When she saw us, she sprinted over.

"Sorry I'm late." she noted. Technically, she was late. But only by a minute and 30 seconds.

"Don't worry, Lewis will be later." I told her in a comforting voice. She sat down and pulled out her blue binder. I wondered if she had any other school supplies besides that old thing.

"Got any ideas?" Dakota asked Joanna, and she nodded reluctantly like she wasn't sure.

"Yo." Lewis greeted simply, looking sweaty despite the freezing weather.

He must have noticed my confused look, because he shrugged and announced, "My pop left without me, so I had to run here." I nodded briefly and leaned my chair on its back legs. "You could warm me up if you'd like." He added, and I shot daggers at him.

"Any ideas?" Dakota asked Lewis, trying to draw the subject away from his friends' douchey behaviour.

"For?"

Dakota scoffed. "The project, dude."

"Ohhhh… no."

I looked at Joanna, giving her the queue to share hers with us. I felt like I did most of my talking with these people without saying a word. And to be honest, I kind of liked that. We communicated through questions, nods, smiles, and sighs. No one demanded any more of me and for that I was grateful.

"I was thinking maybe we could do..." she made a face like she was thinking this one up just now. "Smoking?" She asked us.

Dakota made a face. "I don't know if that really counts as an SJT, even with the loose definition Mr. S" gave us." he told her, and she nodded.

"Jane?" Joanna asked giving me the same look I had given her.

"I was thinking..." I began hopefully "We could do our project on living life to its fullest."

"Like whatcha mean?" Lewis asked, laying his head on the table.

"Like... like working through life obstacles, making mistakes, loving ourselves. All of the things teenagers have so much trouble with." I explained. "We could focus on something like body image or we could do it on a wide spectrum."

Joanna smiled. "I like that. What about you guys?"

"Whatever." Lewis grumbled.

Dakota was silent, so Joanna glanced at his computer screen... and then she punched him in the arm.

"OW... that hurt." Dakota whined.

"This is no time to be playing Skyrim." She reprimanded.

CHAPTER SEVENTEEN –

Can't Help Falling In Love, Elvis.

Joanna and Dakota were nice, and Lewis was civil, but stubborn, the occasional demeaning joke being the only real threat to the peace. He didn't do any work and only opened his mouth to flirt with either me or Joanna. But none the less, I kind of enjoyed them.

We had finally decided on how to format the SJT after three hours of arguing. Joanna wanted to made a video, Lewis made inappropriate jokes about Joanna making a video, and Dakota wanted to do a speech. I liked that idea.

When I got home my mother tried to make me have dinner with her and watch a movie; reminding me that that used to be a daily occurrence. I lied and told her I had gotten dinner after the library, and ran up the stairs to my room. I just hadn't been very hungry lately.

~~~~~~~~~~~~~~~~~~~~~~~~~~~~~~~~~~~

When I woke up the next morning my room was freezing cold and I didn't want to get out of bed.

"Jane!" Mom yelled up the steps, and I groaned in response, my teeth chattering, "Get up!" she demanded.

When I finally did I few minutes later, I realised what it was that had made my room so cold. It had snowed, a lot. But this wasn't unusual for New Jersey. It was always raining, so when it got *this* cold, it was bound to always be snowing.

I pulled on a big red Christmas sweater, deciding not to care that it was only November. It was snowing, which to people in New Jersey, meant it was Christmas.

"Wear your snow boots." my mother reminded me, kissing my temple. Standing next to my 5 foot mother reminded me of how tall I was. She practically had to jump to kiss her daughter on the side of the head. I smiled warmly and gave her a hug, remembering how long it had been since I'd last hugged her, it had been after my first Lilly related nightmare – a few days after the accident. She had held me and calmed me and made me go back to sleep. And she had given me the week off school because of it.

~~~~~~

I didn't have S3 that day, but I did have art. Trisha, as I had learned her to be called, had made a habit of sitting beside me. We talked a lot now. She'd tell bad jokes about nerdy shows and I would laugh and complement her art and ask her all kinds of questions.

Joanna saw me talking to her in the halls and had poked me in the side later, teasing me.

"Someone's got a crush." she teased.

My face went bright red and I had to look down to hide it. "Maybe." I conceded.

Joanna giggled. "Winter formals next month." she told me. "You should ask her."

I thought about it for a moment. "But how do I know if I really like her?"

"Does she make you happy?" Joanna asked.

"Well yeah..."

"And do you get on well?" She continued.

"Yeah." I admitted, my cheeks warming up.

"That's all it takes. She doesn't have to make the world brighter; she's just got to make you brighter." She told me, smiling.

I wanted to ask her, I really did. She was funny, and sweet, and such a great artist, not to mention she was a fabulous listener. I had only ever had one girlfriend before though, so this made me nervous.

"How do I ask?" I questioned, leaning up against a locker, holding my books to my chest.

"Just ask, it doesn't have to be extravagant." Joanna laughed, closing her locker door and smiling at me softly, like she understood. "I might not look it, but I'm pretty shy about that sort of thing myself. I'm kind of hoping Dakota will ask me." she admitted.

Now it was her turn to blush. I gapped at her in shock. Joanna was beautiful, and a straight A student. Dakota was awkward, wore too much hair grease, and was a straight C student. Joanna was on the track team and ate a vegan diet. Dakota played Skyrim and Five Nights at Freddie's and ate at Taco Bell 5 nights a week. They were opposites.

"Opposites attract." she explained, as if reading my mind. "And he's just sweet." she added, sighing and leaning back, hugging her books to her chest and closing her eyes.

"You don't have to wait for him to ask you." I told her.

She nodded. "I know, but I'd rather. I'm kind of afraid he'll say no."

I laughed. I couldn't imagine *Dakota* saying no to *Joanna.*

I didn't think it was possible, but she looked even happier than I had ever seen her. She was beautiful when she smiled, the bigger the better. And if he could make her smile like that, maybe they'd work.

CHAPTER EIGHTEEN –

We're on our Way. Radical Faces.

That day in art, Trisha had been even more friendly than usual, and I had no problem with it.

"Ya know" she told me, a few moments before class ended. "I'm having a party tonight. You should come." I blushed.

"I'd love to be there!" I answered, maybe too quickly.

She giggled lightly and leaned in closely.

"I'd love to see you there." She told me quietly. She was so close that I could feel each breath. She smelled like mint and tea, and for a second I wondered if her mouth tasted that way as well.

I didn't have to wonder long. She pressed her pink lips against mine happily, smiling into my mouth.

She tasted like mint, and tea.

~~~~~~~~~~~~~~~~~~~~~~~~~~~~~~~~

"We're supposed to be working." I reminded Dakota as he chatted to me and Jo about going to see a movie the next time we met up for project work.

"Yeah, babe." Jo agreed. I got the feeling he'd asked her out. They were extremely liberal with the word *babe* but it made Joanna smile, and besides, they could be a whole lot more couple-ish and annoying. He still let me sit directly in front of her at lunch as he sat beside me. Not much had changed.

I wasn't entirely sure when we had started sitting together for lunch. Like I could remember the first day, but I couldn't remember asking to sit with them or being asked. Sometimes it was as if our silent talking continued without us realising it.

"Besides," I added "if we're going to hang out, why would we invite Lewis?"

Dakota shrugged at me as he bit into a McDonald's burger. I couldn't help but wonder if kissing this boy meant Joanna was cheating on her Vegan diet. The boy had 3 milks, 2 burgers, and a large fry. Joanna was munching on salad with olive oil.

"Because, he's a nice guy, he's just dumb. He needs experience dealing with people." He explained lamely.

"He's sexist." Jo countered.

I knew Dakota and Lewis got along in their own respects, they were actually decent friends, but Dakota hated the way Lewis treated women and tried his best to avoid being subject to it.

"And he's an ass." I added, helpfully.

"Do you have an eating disorder?" Dakota asked suddenly. Joanna kicked him under the table.

"Dakota!" she yelled.

"What?" he asked. "She never has lunch and she's been getting so tiny it's a bit worrying."

I felt nervous all the sudden. It was true I hadn't been eating more than a bite of this and a handful of that a day since the accident, but I hadn't thought of it as an eating disorder. Quickly, I tried to change the subject.

"I really don't want to go out with Lewis tonight." I told them "besides I'm going out with Trisha tonight anyway."

"How about this," Dakota suggested. "We'll all meet up at my place tonight and if Trish says yes, stay out all night. Get your freak on."

I snorted at the last part.

"But if she says no and things get awkward, then you come over and join us." He continued.

[76]

"Deal." I agreed.

"And you eat lunch tomorrow." Joanna told me, giving me this look that said *we'll be talking about this.* She wasn't smiling, she looked worried, and I noticed how tired she looked when she wasn't smiling. I felt like I was disappointing her, so I just nodded.

"Sure thing, Jo." I replied reluctantly.

The bell rang and we all exited in different directions, Joanna and Dakota hand and hand until they reached the exit.

CHAPTER NINETEEN –

Karma Police, Radio Head.

Trisha had invited me to her place for a party that night, and I was more nervous than I could handle.

"Who's going to be there?" my mother asked, sitting at my desk stool as I ruffled through drawers for something decent to wear.

"I don't know mom." I sighed. "Just a bunch of underclassmen probably. Trish's a junior."

Mom nodded. Something about them being younger seemed to put her at ease.

"I know you're turning 18 in 2 months and everything," my mother sighed, "but we still have rules. No drinking. I'd rather you stay home if you're going to be drinking."

I nodded, smiling. "No drinking." I agreed. Alcohol tasted like crap to me anyway.

Mom left just as I had found what I was going to wear; a long sleeved black dress shirt, some black skinny jeans, and a little white bowtie. *Just dressy enough* I thought. I wasn't much for dresses but I liked ties quite a lot.

Once I was done getting dressed, I put on my pea coat and clutched the keys to my vehicle. It was a dark red ford pick-up I had inherited when my uncle got an upgrade. It had its dents, but the heat worked and the radio played. And most importantly, it had 4 wheel drive, which I needed for this weather.

It was full force snowing and I cursed New Jersey weather for being so screwy. Two years back there had been two feet of snow on Halloween night.

~~~~~~

When I got to Trish's place, it was packed. The door was unlocked and there was a sign on it that said *'LET YOURSELF IN'* in capitals. I hadn't thought that was a very safe thing to do, but I brushed it off and tried my best not to have an anxiety attack as I pushed through the large crowd. I had planned on asking her to the winter formal that night, and I had it all planned out.

I was going to lead her onto the front porch, shivering closely together as the snow fell and I was going to just tell her exactly how I felt. I loved her smile, and her short hair and tall heels. And I really did think that I could love *her* too. Finally, as I entered what looked like the kitchen, I saw her.

I couldn't breathe.

I couldn't speak.

I couldn't move.

She wasn't alone, not that I had expected her to be all by herself at her own party, but the person she was with was so close to her. A girl much fitter then me, long hair shining healthily, perfect figure in a red dress, was leaning in whispering things into Trisha's ear.

Trisha was giggling that half laugh she did when I would hug her goodbye after talking in the halls, and then she pushed her small stature up to meet the tall stranger and pressed her lips against theirs, and suddenly my feet worked again.

I was running then.

I pushed through crowds, nudging through the groups of dancing teenagers and wondering why I had ever thought I had a chance. I wondered if she kissed all the girls like that, I wondered if I had even meant anything to her.

CHAPTER TWENTY –

The Boy Who Blocked His Own Shot, Brand New,

I would have crashed the car if I left right away, so I laid my head down on the steering wheel and tried to stop crying. I couldn't see through my own tears and mascara was running down my cheeks. The movies lie, crying never looks the way they make it look. *Crying is ugly;* I thought when I caught a glance of myself in the rear-view mirror.

When I finally pulled myself together, I started the car and began driving to Dakotas. I didn't want them to see me like this, so I did my best to wipe the ruined makeup off and hoped my eyes would clear up before I got there.

I had a hard time finding the place, but when I finally got there I saw a small dinky looking house with the shudders hanging off the windows and the roof caving in beneath the thin pile up of snow.

Jo had texted me earlier.

Lewis and I just got to Dakotas, he says text us if you're here. He doesn't want to wake his ma.

I replied.

I'm out front.

A few moments later, Dakotas lanky form appeared in a now open door way. He looked like slenderman in the dark.

When I got up to the door, he held it open for me and nodded up the stairs.

"Jo's up there. Lewis is in the kitchen making us popcorn." He had an understanding look in his eyes.

I knew it was obvious. I bet he just thought she said no to going to the dance with me and I had taken it too badly to stick around. Jo was the only one who knew that she had kissed me in the first place.

When I got up the stairs, Jo was leaning against the head board of a futon and eating some weird looking vegan chips. She smiled when she saw me in the door way, but then he smile turned into a pout.

"She said no." Joanna stated, like it was a fact.

"Didn't ask." I told her. She had given me the most confused look then, and I knew I had to explain.

"She was kissing someone else." I told her, and I spotted Lewis walking up the stairs behind me. I moved out of the door way to let him in.

"*I* could kiss you." He offered cockily.

BAM.

I smacked him hard across the face and he nearly dropped the bowl of popcorn he had been holding. At first, I thought he might hit me back. He grabbed me and pulled me up to him and then he seemed to of thought better of it and let me fall to the floor.

"I'm sick of your sexist attitude!" I screamed "Why are you even here?" I continued. "It's obvious you don't like us!"

He looked angry, but hurt. "I do like you guys!" he insisted. "I like *you* a lot."

I was angry, so angry about so many things and I just couldn't handle this asshole at the moment.

"Well you sure as hell suck at showing it!" I yelled, and now Dakota and Joanna were sitting on the futon watching us. Dakota nodded in the corner of my eye as if reluctantly agreeing with a church sermon.

"I was flirting." He explained lamely.

"You're always flirting; you're hitting on girls who don't want you anywhere near them. You catcall, you trash talk, and you **piss me off!**"

He looked like a stunned deer in head lights standing there in front of me, just barely holding onto the bowl in his hands.

"I'm," he stuttered out "I'm sorry." I frowned. He deserved to hear this, I knew that. But he could have heard in a number of more level headed ways.

"It's ok." I explained. "I mean it's not okay, but, you just need to work on it, okay?" I asked.

He nodded feebly and helped me up, holding the bowl of popcorn out to me as a peace offering, cracking open a fresh cocky smile.

I had so many emotions boxing one another; I wasn't in any mood to smile back. I didn't know what to do, and I wished Lilly was around to give me a little advice.

I was quickly realising something. *To quote Tyler Knott Gregson,* I thought. *there is a lot more to life than simply surviving it.*

CHAPTER TWENTYONE –
Flaws, Bastille,

Once the anger and frustration of me and Lewis's argument had deflated, we both joined the others on the futon. I don't know why I didn't just leave and go home, but something about this group project made it feel like we *had* to learn to deal with one another.

"So what happened at the party?" Dakota asked, scooting closer.

"I don't want to talk about it." I told him, looking down. "It's embarrassing. We all have to keep our secrets, ya know?"

Dakota laughed. "No we don't." He countered.

"I don't know everything about you."

"What do you want to know?"

I thought for a moment, leaning my head on Jo's shoulder. She laid her head on mine.

"Your deepest secret, one none of us know. If you all share your secrets, I'll share mine." I gathered.

"And…" Lewis jeered, and I noticed how lightly he poked me. He was afraid of screwing up again.

"And I'll tell you what happened tonight."

"Good." they said in unison.

"Who wants to go first?" I asked. I suddenly realised how childish we were all being, and I wondered if they noticed too. We looked like a bunch of 6th graders playing truth or dare. But it felt nice.

"I volunteer as tribute!" Jo busted out, picking up her head.

I smiled and turned to her. "Go ahead."

"Okay, okay, okay. I got this." She began, taking a big breath.

Jo laid down her arm palm up on the bed and pulled the sleeve of her sweater to her elbow. Her wrist was littered with scars.

There was a row of sighs and Dakota bent to kiss her wrist. "I haven't cut since freshmen year." Jo explained, licking her lips. "I met some nice people who gave me confidence in who I am. I'm not just the Asian American girl in the back of the room." She sighed then, like she was about to cry, but her smile widened. "I'm Joanna Lee."

Dakota hugged Jo and smiled.

[86]

"I'll go next." Lewis offered, and I nodded.

"I've never had an actual girlfriend." He admitted sullenly. "Girls will sleep with me, but no one wants to be with me." Dakota poked him in the arm.

"Sorry dude. But it's probably because of how you treat them." I could tell he was struggling not to use a *we told you so'* voice.

"Yeah." Lewis agreed surprisingly, and he looked up at me like a big jockish puppy, then at Jo. "I know that now."

Lewis looked a little bit like a kid who's just starting to realize how much his parents do for him. He looked at me and Jo with a new respect, but I knew this would take quite a bit to get through his head.

"Okay Dakota, your turn." I giggled, and he shrugged.

"I'm an open book." He announced. "Nothing to admit."

Jo pierced him with one of her most dominant looks, smile dropping into a smirk. "C'mon babe." she coxed.

I poked Dakota in the side and nodded. "You built this confessional." I reminded him.

"Fine." He conceded. "Uhhh, okay, I stole my laptop." He admitted.

I gasped loudly. He stole an Alienware? Kid was good. Lilly would be proud of his ninja skills.

"Yikes bro." Lewis laughed. "Nice."

Dakota laughed a little. "I feel pretty bad about it." He conceded. "Your turn Jane!"

I looked down at my hands and shrugged. "Um, well, my friend Lilly passed away last month." I told them, and they all frowned. "She was driving home after dropping me off and she hit some ice and..."

I was speaking too fast, too quiet. "I have these horrible dreams. I can't sleep or eat, and tonight at the party Trish was kissing another girl, and I don't get it. Did it mean anything to her when she kissed me?"

Jo's frown slowly dissipated into her usual smile. "She needs a hug, and a subway sandwich wouldn't hurt either." she announced. "Let's get her boys."

Jo tackled me first, followed by the other two, and I was lucky I could even breathe under their weight.

"Ya know." Lewis started from above us; "Our confessions should go in our SJT project." we hummed in agreement, and then burst out laughing.

"You know what we should do?" I asked them.

"What?" they asked in unison.

"Go hiking." I answered.

They were crazy, I thought. *Good crazy.*

So maybe I didn't know how long it was going to take for Lewis to understand how to interact with females properly, and I didn't know what I was going to do when I saw Trisha at school, and I didn't know if I would ever be hungry again.

But under these people, these friends, surrounded in love and laughter and stupidity, I tried to figure out the perfect way to describe the emotion I was feeling.

I know I thought *this is euphoria.*

EPILOGUE

Exitlude, The Killers

CONCLUSION:

In conclusion, if there is one thing we can be sure of it is that we are not perfect. We are those who fall victim to our own emotions and allow ourselves to be undone by hard times. We all still have so much to learn.

And if there are two things in which we can be sure of, and I am aware that that is setting the bar quite high, that is that the only thing that is constant is change. Life will always throw us things we feel we cannot handle, but there is never going to be anything we can't fix. Or at least, tape together.

THANK YOU

SONG LIST/TABLE OF CONTENTS –

Before) Just Like Heaven, The Cure,

Prologue) Enterlude, The Killers,

1) Back Then, B-Story,

2) 1979, Smashing Pumpkins,

3) Sick Muse, Metric,

4) Here I Land, Nicholas Stevenson,

5) Wonderwall, Oasis,

6) Outgrown, Best Left Unsaid,

7) Jesus Christ, Brand New,

8) The Night I Drove Alone, Citizen,

9) Of a Friday Night, Anaïs Mitchell,

10) Brothers on a Hotel Bed, Death Cab for Cutie,

11) Too Much Time, John Vanderslice,

12) At Least I Have Nothing, Saints Motel,

13) Kill a Hipster, Watsky

14) Walls, Oklahoma Car Crash,

15) Come on Eileen, Dexys Midnight Runners,

16) Sloppy Seconds, Watsky,

17) Can't Help Falling In Love, Elvis,

18) We're on our Way, Radical Faces,

19) Karma Police, Radio Head,

20) The Boy Who Blocked His Own Shot, Brand New,

21) Flaws, Bastille,

Epilogue) Exitlude, The Killers,

Where to find me: Tumblr and YouTube @MarvelousMacey